
SIBLING RIVALRY

The Case of the Disputed Inheritance

BUTTERS PI

RORI BLEU

ROSIE CHAPEL

First printing: 2025
ISBN: 978-1-7644985-2-4 (ebook)
ISBN: 978-1-7644985-3-1 (paperback)

Ulfire Pty. Ltd.
P.O. Box 1481
South Perth
WA 6951
Australia

Cover Design: Rebecca Norman
Images Courtesy: Canva and Deposit Photos
Designed in Canva using appropriate licences.

❋ Formatted with Vellum

SIBLING RIVALRY
Butters P.I.

*"Down these mean streets a man must go who is not himself mean,
who is neither tarnished nor afraid.
The detective must be a complete man and a common man and yet
an unusual man.
He must be, to use a rather weathered phrase, a man of honor—by
instinct, by inevitability, without thought of it, and certainly
without saying it.
He must be the best man in his world and a good enough man for
any world."*

The Simple Art of Murder
Raymond Chandler

CHAPTER ONE

1942 - San Francisco

June 1942. Not only was America hip deep in a war which encompassed half the planet, but also, and more fortuitously, had won a major battle in the Pacific at Midway against the Japanese Imperial Navy.

In the months leading up to the victory, troops were moved in and out of San Francisco on their way to the Pearl Harbor naval base at O'ahu, and points west.

'Frisco had, for want of a better description, become the Grand Central Station of the US military, their numbers almost, but not quite, overshadowing the disparate quota of unsavory characters lurking on the fringes of the city, whose intent was far less… laudable.

The waterfront was rife with gangsters, spies, and small-time criminals, intent on making the most out of skimming war materials and cashing in on humanity's confusion.

As for me… none of that mattered.

I flipped through my paper, remembering cheery days spent in a muddy trench during the last war, before returning to my beloved City by the Bay, where I was a detective for ten years.

A flourishing career arrested, to coin a phrase, when the SFPD in general, and yours truly in particular, became mired in allegations of graft and corruption. Regrettably, while not a single one relating to me were substantiated, my claims of innocence went unheeded. As far as the brass was concerned, they had their scapegoat.

Fortuitously, my then lover seduced me into believing we could set up shop as private detectives. Although sceptical, I trusted her instincts and Butters PI came into being. The fact she ditched me for some sleazy mobster, leaving me in the lurch is neither here nor there. Resentful? Sore? *Me?* Never…

My stroll down memory lane was interrupted by a loud rap on my door. A shapely silhouette through the frosted glass announced my next prospective client was awaiting an invitation to enter.

"Come in." *No one pays me to be a bellhop.*

The door swung open to reveal a beautiful, bleached blonde. Without so much as a *Hello, Detective, my life is in danger,* she sashayed into my office, settled in the chair at the opposite side of my desk, and dropped what looked like a carpet bag by her feet. Its faded appearance at odds with her aura of wealth and elegant sophistication.

Interesting. The hairs on the back of my neck prickled.

With studied nonchalance, she plucked a cigarette from a sterling silver case. Tapping the end on the metal, packing the tobacco tightly like a pro, she slipped it between her Hollywood-starlet red lips.

Without uttering a word, she sat there, fingers drumming on the arm of the chair impatiently. Apparently, my visitor expected me to get off my ass to light her Chesterfield.

Fighting the frown hovering at her entitled attitude, I contemplated exercising my ego and telling her there was no smoking in my office but her baby-blues were too enticing to ignore. So, I took the bait.

Rounding the cluttered desk, I rifled in my pocket for my lighter. Standing in front of her, I snapped it open casually, hitting that one-in-a-million chance of it coming to life instantly. I leaned against the edge of the desk and, with exaggerated patience, held the tiny flame under the tip of her cigarette.

"Ya know, doll, I don't let just anyone smoke in my place," I remonstrated, keeping my tone mild as I watched her inhale languidly.

"Does that make me special?" She breathed out, arching a cool brow; the faintest hint of a condescending smile curving her mouth. A coil of burnt tobacco, the aroma redolent of Stella's noxious Turkish brand, created a fleeting veil between us and memories teased threatening to distract.

I squashed the sharp pang with effort. "No, being a Wentworth does that," I replied bluntly. "To what do I owe the pleasure of a visit from one of the city's elite?"

At this, her coy composure crumbled. An ugly wrinkle furrowed her forehead, distorting her beautiful face.

"Mr. Butters, my sister is m—" she began.

"It's Butterfield," I corrected.

"Excuse me?"

"The name is Jacob Butterfield."

"But the name on your door—"

"A souvenir from a disgruntled and incompetent door artist. It serves as an ironic reminder that a finished job, no matter the outcome, is better than not getting it done at all."

My potential client smirked. "In other words, you're too cheap to have it redone?"

"Let's just say frugal."

There was no sense explaining that, as a result, everyone in the Greater San Francisco area referred to me as Butters. To change it now, would be like changing who I am... and, yes, I'm too cheap.

"Instead of beating about the bush, how about you tell me how you found my agency, and why?"

"Mr. Butterfield, I'm terribly anxious about my younger sister, Pamela. She was supposed to meet her boyfriend at some seedy gin joint on the Waterfront two days ago, and I haven't heard from her since. I fear she may have fallen into trouble or worse, *eloped* with the lowlife."

Her delicate shudder and horrified tone mirrored her expression, which was the perfect blend of distraught and irate... yet somehow her flawless complexion managed to remain unmarred by a single wrinkle.

This didn't answer my question but, although innately suspicious of theatrics, I set that to one side... *don't jump to conclusions, Butters...* and circled back to my side of the desk. Taking a semi-crushed pack of smokes from the suit coat draped over the back of my chair, I lit one, letting the cloud of smoke drift lazily upwards. "How do I fit into your game of hide and seek?"

"I asked around the docks whether there was a private investigator trustworthy enough to find her," the elder Wentworth sibling laid on the charm with a trowel.

"Okay, Miss Wentworth, skip the fairytale and tell me the truth."

I suspected she thought I was another uneducated gorilla who could not read, much like the muscled suit photographed trailing behind her when she left the Federal Court House.

A photograph which was splashed across every major newspaper in the country, along with the accompanying tale of woe between Vanessa and Pamela Wentworth.

Neither did the sisters hide the fact they bore no love for

each other, thanks, in part, to the multimillion-dollar inheritance their late father had left them, and the fact they had different mothers.

Five years older than her half-sister, Vanessa, the only child of their father's first marriage was left motherless at the age of seven. The younger daughter, Pamela, was the result of an extra-marital tryst with a maid no longer in the picture.

If the gossip columns were to be believed — and I never missed a single issue because that was where the juiciest details could be found — twenty-seven-year old Pamela, apparently resolved not to have her independence curtailed by a wedding ring seemed bound and determined to live every day as if it were her last.

Decadent parties, a new man every week, spending money like water. In all honesty, her extravagant, pleasure-seeking behaviour was no more or less sensational than that of her peers. Flouting the rules was regarded as a rite of passage, especially among the fast set, except Pamela did not have the luxury of anonymity.

Her hedonistic lifestyle was curbed when, in the old man's haste to check out of this world, he neglected to specify in his will *how* the money was to be divided, tying up the funds in probate.

Adding insult to injury, as always seemed to be the case in these messy situations, a mysterious second will materialized, leaving everything to the older daughter should the younger be proved mentally unstable.

Unwittingly playing into her sister's plan, Pamela's frequent and very public displays of wilful recklessness had all but handed Vanessa the diagnosis on a finely engraved silver platter… no plain flatware for this family.

The press was having a field day with the animosity between the siblings.

Taking a drag on her cigarette, the end burning as red-hot as the glare she gave me, Vanessa let the smoke roll out of her mouth on a huff.

"Fine, long story short, I need you to find her. Hopefully in one piece."

"Why don't you go to the police? Missing people fall under their jurisdiction."

"Because if she turns up dead, I'll be the only suspect."

CHAPTER TWO

"Point taken. I'm sure my fee of fifty dollars a day, plus expenses, won't be a problem?" I observed politely.

"Find her in one piece and I'll double it."

Ignoring all rational arguments to the contrary, I took a leap of faith, unable to decipher whether I wanted Vanessa where I could keep an eye on her or for other, less… gallant reasons.

"Probably unnecessary but, until we get to the bottom of this, you could be in danger. If, indeed, your sister has met with foul play, you might be next on the list. For the time being, I think you ought to keep a low profile. Am I correct in presuming this is something you have already considered?" I jerked my head at the bag next to her chair. She nodded slowly.

"I know somewhere safe. It's not much, but neither is it crawling with cops, or bad guys."

Vanessa studied her surroundings dubiously.

I chuckled, "Doll, I'd never think of hiding you here. I have an even seedier place in mind, but I can guarantee no one will find you there.

Reluctantly, she agreed, admitting she had packed a few things on the assumption it might be prudent to avoid the spotlight for a while. This played neatly into my hands because the last thing I needed to be associated with was a dead or kidnapped heiress.

I dropped her off at the apartment of one Esmeralda Harper, my crotchety landlady with a questionable drinking problem. She may enjoy a tipple too many, but Mrs Harper is a canny soul and not fooled easily, reading between the lines when asked to shelter Miss Wentworth.

To her credit, Vanessa made no comment about the humble interior. I imagined it was a far cry from the opulence she was used to. That said, Esmerelda had a good eye, and possessed some beautiful furnishings, the refined decor never failing to surprise me. Perhaps it was not the worst place to spend a couple of days.

A promise to supply copious amounts of rum in exchange for babysitting fees not only forestalled any protest she might be formulating, but also had the added benefit of mollifying her somewhat, and I left them to become acquainted.

Pondering my next move, I decided a visit to the SFPD's Southern Station, which just so happened to be my old stomping ground, might prove fruitful.

Built in the '20s in a Spanish Baroque style, it was the antithesis of the original premises on 4th and Clara, and its grandeur made me laugh, bearing in mind the excessive amount of money wasted on it could have been put to better use. For over a decade, I was proud to walk its corridors.

Ascending the stairs to the second floor, I wandered into the province of the Homicide Squad. In the back office, hunched over his desk, sat my former partner, Louis Mazzetti, except he had been promoted from lieutenant to captain.

Without knocking, I entered his domain, tossed my hat on his desk, and made myself comfortable in one of his plush leather chairs.

Without looking up from his papers, Mazzetti growled, "Butters…" Needless to state, that name stalks me everywhere, "…you're not welcome here."

"Come on, Lou, is that anyway to treat your old partner?"

It was the man on the other side of the desk who had put the finger on me… to save his own skin. He accepted bribes from the local brothels to turn a blind eye to their operations, even after a couple of girls, Mae Oliver and June Davis, ended up in the Bay.

Despite the fact, they were found in a rented Ford Coupe, ten feet from the wharf, still strapped into their seats… the coroner — a couple of inexplicable anomalies aside — was unable to find evidence to the contrary and ruled the cause as death by drunk driving. Word on the street claimed they were victims of a burgeoning gang war.

When the Feds stepped in to investigate, I suspect my erstwhile partner, then Lieutenant Mazzetti — although he denied it even after I was escorted from the building, forcibly — whispered into someone's ear that I knew both women, intimately, and might have more information about the war than I had disclosed.

Pissed off because I had confronted him about taking bribes, Mazzetti compounded his sins by dropping me in the shit with some evidence he had planted at the scene, in the shape of a brick of hashish.

Mud sticks and, despite the fact the Feds, eventually, connected Mae and June's deaths to two murders in China-town, my credibility was blown to smithereens.

His guilt made him ever-so compliant to my requests for information.

"My old partner, no, but an unscrupulous Private Dick, that's another story."

"Wash your mouth out, Mazzetti. My scruples are clean, so cut the attitude."

"And you can cut the bull, Jake," Mazzetti lifted his head to look me in the eye. "To what do I owe the displeasure of your visit?"

"I wanted to congratulate you on the promotion…"

That earned a skeptical eye roll. "And?" he pressed.

"…to ask whether your men in blue have fished any more bodies out of the water recently, specifically around The Embarcadero?"

Blowing a resigned sigh, Mazzetti thumbed through his morning paperwork. He stopped and handed me a sheet with a photo attached to it. The report was dated two days ago.

"Nothing around the docks, but this one was dredged up from beneath the Golden Gate."

The face in the picture looked as though it had absorbed the full impact of hitting the water and was barely recog-nizable.

According to the coroner's report, given no witnesses had come forward to pinpoint the moment she swan-dived off the bridge, time of death could not be gaged with precision. His ruling: To be determined… *probable* suicide.

Doesn't anyone die of natural causes anymore? I thought peevishly.

Out loud, I inquired, while continuing to read, "Any idea who she was?"

"Not for sure, but the guys investigating the scene found a purse belonging to—"

I broke in, "Let me guess, Pamela Wentworth?"

Mazzetti's eyes narrowed. "How on earth did you know that?"

"Lucky guess?"

"Not hardly," Mazzetti contradicted. "Answer the question, Butterfield."

"Let's just say a concerned citizen was looking for her. Anyway, about the purse, don't you think it's discovery is a little too convenient?"

"Hell, who knows what goes through the brain of somebody set on taking their life. Well, maybe with the exception of a bullet," Mazzetti sniped sarcastically.

"Hey, respect for the dead," I admonished. "Seriously, do you think your suicide is the Wentworth girl?"

"The physical description, height, and weight fits but I'm not prepared to state it categorically until I talk to the sister. You don't happen to know where I might find her do you? I've reached out but only managed to speak to her bodyguard. Let's hope he has the brains to pass on the message," Mazzetti finished morosely.

"Good luck with that, and nope, just what I read in the gossip columns," I supplied breezily.

"Butters, if I find you're hiding a potential material witness, I'll forget we were friends and toss you into—"

"Yeah, yeah, a hole so deep I'll never see the light of day again."

Leaving the station, I considered swinging by the docks, but the word dock changed my mind. Instead, I pointed the DeSoto in the opposite direction towards the City Morgue, hoping to have a chat with the friendly neighborhood ghoul, Coroner Hamilton Washington.

I made sure to call in at Hamilton's favorite deli to pick up a pastrami on rye. The good coroner was much more cooperative on a full stomach.

Coming to a halt in one of the parking spaces assigned to visitors, the macabre irony of the sign elicited a dry chuckle. I pegged this as *Drop Off Only*.

No matter how painstakingly the city had worked to conceal the identity of this place, the miasma of death clung to it like a shroud and, as I approached the glass entrance, force of habit compelled me to rub menthol under my nose to mask it.

I followed the hallway to Hamilton's office, hoping to find him there to avoid the repugnant descent to the bowels of hell.

My luck held.

CHAPTER THREE

Knocking on the frame of his open door, I was greeted by a man who looked as though he ought to have retired years ago. That said, Hamilton claimed the dead haunted him at home in his sleep, so working with them was a better alternative.

Quote: *"Less Scary."*

"Ah, Sergeant Butterfield." No matter how many times I reminded him I was no longer on force, he persisted in addressing me as such. Finally, I gave up.

"To what do I owe this visit?" his question echoing Mazzetti's. He stopped and sniffed the air. Like a hunting dog, Hamilton's nose was attuned to unusual smells, probably why he was so good at his job, yet he was able to filter out the foulest odors. "With pastrami from Max's Delicatessen, no less. This must be important."

"What? Can't I call in on a friend and bring lunch?"

The coroner and I enjoyed something akin to a love-hate relationship. On one hand, for those of us who had no choice, observing an autopsy was ghoulish in the extreme, on the other, it was often the coroner's finding which could provide the breakthrough in a case.

The morning Mae and June were fished out of San Francisco Bay reared up in my mind. Hamilton's initial, and to me almost flippant, report had rankled, particularly because he seemed to toe the establishment's preconceived line regarding their deaths.

When the Feds assumed jurisdiction of the investigation and, reluctantly, saw fit to question the findings in light of two other murders, Hamilton redeemed himself and, since then, had made up for the *misinterpretation* in spades.

He raised an eyebrow at my comment. "Bullshit, Butters." His rebuttal did not stop him from reaching out to snatch the sandwich. Wasting one of Max's creations was a cardinal sin.

Settling back, he tore into the thick sandwich with the veracity of a rabid hyena.

Waving his hand at the empty chair across from him, he blurted out around a mouth full of food, "Urr no yoinin' me?" Which I deciphered as a question as to why I was not eating with him.

"Ya know this place kills my appetite."

"Rookie." Hamilton chuckled, biting a large chunk of sandwich. "Now, you were about to tell me why you brought me lunch."

"Mazzetti told me a body came in over the weekend. Any idea who she was?"

"Nah," Hamilton said, wiping his mouth on his sleeve.

I did *not* want to know what else had touched that piece of clothing.

"No. No ID on her, but I'm sure Mazzetti's report already told you that."

"Was she a jumper?" I asked.

"Oh, God no. She was dead before she went over the railing."

"You sure? Your preliminary report said probable suicide. Wouldn't the associated injuries have been sustained from the fall?"

"Not like this, and the reason we do autopsies on atypical deaths. Follow me down and I'll show you."

So much for luck... but who was I to disappoint the coroner?

We trudged down to the ice box known as the Morgue. Stepping through the double doors, Hamilton flipped a switch, and the overhead fluorescent lights blinked and buzzed to life.

Several empty gurneys lined up neatly were draped with clean oilcloths in readiness, while a handful provided a temporary resting place for incumbents awaiting their final disposition.

Hamilton clomped across the tiled floor to one of the examination tables. The sheet covering the body was marred by water stains.

Our jumper.

Unceremoniously, he flung the sheet back to expose a dark-haired woman whose skin exhibited a blue-ish hue. Her torso was splayed open from below her chin to the apex of her thighs.

The coroner took a probe and began his biology lesson.

"If you look in the tray behind you, you will see this girl's lungs. Unlike your friends..." His reference to the supposed accidental drowning of Mae and June, later proved to be murder, led to an awkward pause. Clearing his throat, he continued, "...there is no water in her lungs."

"So? Just means she died on impact, doesn't it?"

He pointed to a small bone located in her throat. "This is the hyoid. It's a fascinating bone, the only one in the entire body classed as free-floating because it is disarticulated, instead it is held in place by soft tissue. See how it's broken on both sides? Proves she was strangled and then tossed into the bay. Any chance this is your missing person? I would love to ID her."

"Christ, Hamilton, I don't even know who I'm looking for exactly," I lied. "I can't confirm whether they are one and the same."

"Someone showed up earlier, inquiring about her."

"Really? You have a description, or better yet a name?"

"A description? No. I was out on a call when they came in. As for a name. I have one, but I doubt it will help."

Hamilton handed me a log book with a name circled. Miss Joan Doe.

"So, Jane here's her sister?" I said, unable to hide my sarcasm.

"Could be but whoever it was left no instructions as to what to do with the body."

"Thanks, Hamilton," I said as I beat a hasty retreat from the morgue. "I owe you one."

"More like twenty-one, Butterfield, but who's counting?"

I toyed with the idea of taking the scenic route home by way of The Embarcadero, but the day was almost over, and I did not have the energy to elbow my way through a crowd of boozed-up sailors and dockworkers wetting their collective whistles, on the off-chance of getting the information I wanted.

Better to wait until tomorrow when the crowds were less… inebriated and the barman more… amenable.

Decision made, I drove home via Clara's where I whiled away a good hour in relative peace as I munched my way through plate of fried chicken accompanied by a mug of coffee so strong, I could feel it in my finger tips.

My landlady's altruism in mind, I ordered a pile of food to take home and hauled my weary butt back to my apartment building.

Esmerelda and Vanessa greeted me with barely concealed tolerance and sulky resignation respectively. A match made in heaven this was not.

The tantalising aroma of hot food appeased them somewhat and we managed to get through the evening without even a whisper of a temper tantrum… from any of us.

I called that a win.

It was nearly midnight when I trudged up the stairs and crawled into bed. In spite of my exhaustion, sleep was hard won that night. I had the gnawing suspicion this case had the potential to get considerably more complicated.

In view of what was about to happen, maybe I ought to consider a sideline as a medium.

To my annoyance, I woke late, very late, and felt like a wrung out dishcloth. Couldn't blame the beer, I only had one, determined to keep my wits about me while in the company of the two women in my landlady's apartment.

Not naive enough to think they would become bosom buddies, civility is not restricted to class or wealth. Yes, my idea might turn out to be a huge mistake but it was the best I had for now, so they would just have to grin and bear it.

Sluggishly, I dragged myself out of bed, indulged in a cursory wash, got dressed, and drove back to Clara's for desperately needed sustenance.

Serving me my usual, albeit belated, breakfast, Clara

studied my rumpled appearance speculatively and announced I needed a woman.

"I have two," I groaned.

"Two?" Her eyebrows shot under her greying hairline. "What have I missed?"

I chuckled and some of the tension left my body. "Nothing like that." I gave Clara a potted account of the case.

"And you left an heiress with Esme?" she exclaimed. "Are you crazy?"

"It was the only place I could think of where no one would look," I replied sheepishly.

Shaking her head, Clara wiped her hands on a towel. "Don't come crying to me when it all goes to hell in a hand basket," she cautioned sagely, and went to serve another customer.

Swilling the bacon and eggs down with my second coffee of the day, I dropped a bill on the counter, waved at Clara and left, her "watch your back," following me through the door.

CHAPTER FOUR

Yielding to the inevitable, I pressed my foot on the accelerator, prayed the caffeine would kick in sooner rather than later, and drove to The Embarcadero.

My least favorite section of San Francisco.

Parking my DeSoto in front of a dive frequented by some of the seedier members of our fair city, I surveyed my surroundings.

A couple of young sailors in their dress whites, presumably on liberty from their ship, were leaving the joint.

A group of stevedores passed them on their way in from the docks.

Climbing out of the car. I followed the stevedores, eaves-dropping on their conversation. The bulk was standard crap: beef with the union shop steward, unfair management practices, too many ships to load and unload and not enough days to do so.

The youngest-looking member of the group brought all other topics to a halt when he asked, "Did anyone else see the pegs on that dish poking around the docks this morning?"

"I saw her." One of the older guys shrugged. "'Prolly a working girl looking for some poor swabbie to fleece."

"Are you nuts?" the kid refuted scornfully "Did you see her clothes? Way too posh for a hooker. 'Sides, I heard her asking around about the Dutchman, proper hoity toity she sounded. Why the hell do you think she would be looking for that old fossil?"

Another chimed in, "Who knows and who cares. Odds are, we'll find her off one of the piers in the morning floating face-down."

Grudgingly, I acknowledged the guy was probably right. Seemed it was not a good day unless a body or three bobbed up on the Bay's sands.

As for the Dutchman… what would prompt anyone, other than a hardened criminal, to come all the way out to The Embarcadero to find a washed-up forger?

At one time, Levi Van Dijk was the personal money generator for Frank Lanza, San Francisco's gang boss. Van Dijk produced bills which rivaled those printed by the US government.

When his currency began flooding the West Coast, J. Edgar Hoover took personal charge of tracking down the source. It cost the Dutchman a dime in Alcatraz when he was caught.

There were rumors from the Rock that his last act of forgery was creating his own parole paperwork, but no one was about to own up to the fact he had walked out through the front door of his own volition.

As the longshoremen made their way to the rear of the saloon, I bellied up to the bar.

Behind the worn wooden counter stood the joint's owner, Oscar Bartholomew, with whom I had had run-ins on more than one occasion when on the force. Needless to state, there was no love lost between us.

"Well, if it isn't Detective Butterfield of the SFPD. You drowned any more hookers lately, Sergeant?"

At times like this, I was glad I was no longer a police officer because what I did next was frowned on by the upper echelon.

Chuckling along with the chowderhead, I reached over the bar, grabbed Bartholomew by his cheap tie, and slammed his face on the counter.

No longer laughing, he yelped in pain, "I-I was kidding, Butters. You know me, always with the jokes."

Yanking my gun from its holster, I used it to tickle his left ear. "Yeah, yeah, you're a real comedian. Lucky for you, I'm in a good mood, Bartholomew, and am prepared to give you the chance to keep your ear."

"An-anything, Sergeant. J-just ask."

"The Dutchman. Where can I find him?"

"I-I don't know who you're talkin—"

I cocked the hammer. "Think carefully, Bartholomew."

"Yeah, yeah… the Dutchman. It's like I told the woman this morning—"

"Woman? What woman?"

"I have no idea who she is. Never seen her around before."

"My patience is running thin, Oscar. Describe her."

"I don't know. A stunner, well-dressed. She flashed cash for the info."

"And what did you tell her?" I pressed.

"The last I heard, he was staying in the old harbor master's shack."

"Is there anything else you want to share?" It wasn't a serious question, more a curiosity.

Wriggling free, Bartholomew whined, "If I see you in my joint again, I'll gut ya like a flounder, that's if the Dutchman doesn't beat me to it."

"Always a delight, Oscar." I snorted derisively.

Driving to the shack. I passed row upon row of berths filled with all types of military transports, warships, or cargo vessels. Each flying the *Stars and Stripes*, ready to remind Japanese Admiral Yamamoto that his cowardly attack on Pearl Harbor only succeeded in awakening a sleeping giant.

Regardless of who started the war, San Francisco was definitely profiting from it.

Turning my attention to the matter at hand, I cruised to a halt, a judicious distance from the Dutchman's workshop, alighted, and approached with caution. Even through the closed door, the unmistakeable odor of printers' chemicals seared my nostrils.

I guess you **are** *back in business again, old man.* I knocked… *no harm being polite.*

"Go away," a crotchety voice with a distinct accent, bellowed from inside.

"Dutchman, open up." I thought I would get a better response if I had the forger believe I was still a cop. "It's Detective Butterfield. I've a couple of questions for you," adding sweetly, "if you would be so kind."

To my surprise, the old fool cracked the door, and peered out.

"The Butterfield I know got his ass fired from the force," he grumbled. "So, beat it."

He tried to force the door shut but, anticipating the move, I slid my foot between it and the frame, feeling my former dress shoe scuff up even more. I made a mental note to add the cost of a new pair of wingtips to Vanessa Wentworth's invoice… and not a cheap pair from Woolworth's either!

I put my shoulder against the aging wooden paneling and shoved hard. The door creaked alarmingly under the pressure and Van Dijk's strength impressed me, but it was not enough to bar my entry.

"Come now, is that any way to greet an old friend, Levi?" I reproached as he gave in and let the door swing open. "I doubt many of your old gang are willing to travel out here to visit… or are still alive for that matter."

"I got nothing to discuss with you, Butters."

"Really?" I asked as I wandered to an old printing press set up on a table. I toyed with it, the printheads smacking against each other with no paper to buffer the impact.

"Stop it, you fool. You'll damage the plates," the Dutchman yelled, grabbing me from behind, and wrenching me away from the crank. Even with the weight of the press, we nearly upended it.

Van Dijk released me to steady his precious printer. He checked for any damage then spun to face me. "Use your ears, Butterfield, I Have Nothing To Say To You." Jabbing me in the chest with a stained finger on each word in emphasis.

I batted aside his weathered hand. "Not even about your illegal side business? The government not providing enough in your old age?"

"Shut up, gumshoe. If I *was* doing anything illegal, which I am not admitting to, there's nothing you can do. From what I heard, you'd have trouble getting anyone to believe you anyway. Get lost before I call the real cops."

"You're behind the times, Levi. I might be a gumshoe, but I'm legit, so please… go ahead. I'm sure they would love to see what you are up to. Answering my questions would be a lot easier. All I want to know is who hired you?"

Picking up a length of pipe, the Dutchman banged it on the table, then brandished it in my face. "Last warning, Butterfield, before I bash your ugly mug into next week."

I tipped my hat. "Fine, but don't think I won't be back."

I skirted the angry old man, making sure not to turn my

back on him. At the door, I reached for and grasped the knob from behind and slipped out.

Aggrieved at my failure to garner anything of value, I stalked to my car and perched on the bumper mulling over my next move, while the balmy breeze cleared my head of the noxious fumes which seemed to leach from the crumbling walls of the Shack.

Letting my thoughts roam unchecked, I stayed there for several minutes, admiring the view across the Bay until the, refreshingly, salty tang supplanted the foul odour.

Aware I had nothing to gain by loitering on the docks at this hour, I elected to broaden my education.

The library was a veritable repository of newspapers and I had a friend… yes, a friend, get your mind out of the gutter… sheesh… who was always willing to rummage through the archives. I needed to read everything I could find pertaining to the Wentworth family.

I spent a productive hour or so scouring the neat pile of newspapers supplied by the ever-helpful Edna.

By the time I folded the last one, and returned them to the desk as requested, while no closer to unraveling the mystery surrounding the supposed disappearance of Pamela Wentworth, my understanding of the family's turbulent history and ongoing hostility had increased ten-fold.

The fact I wanted to go home and soak in hot bath was testament to how grubby the excesses of the rich and famous made me feel.

I called it a day. It behoved me to check in at my office before I checked on Vanessa.

Hers was not my only case.

CHAPTER FIVE

Entering the scruffy building, I climbed the four flights, spotting my afternoon copy of the *Chronicle* on the threshold awaiting my return. I stooped to pick it up, bumping the door in the process. Magically, it popped open.

I frowned, and listened through the gap, startled when the screech of chair legs scraping across the wooden floor reached my ears.

My recent internal debate rearing up in my mind, I drew my .38 snub-nose revolver from my ankle holster — in my line of business one can never be over-armed — and tiptoed inside.

On a chair, bathed in a brilliant rainbow, courtesy of the afternoon sunlight through the stained glass, stood a petite brunette, her incredible legs accentuated by her neat, polka dot dress. Focused on searching my cupboards, it seemed my arrival had gone unheard.

I had no need to ask her name because I had seen her picture splashed across the papers with her sister. The very same sister I had met this morning, frantically hunting for my current intruder.

Without turning, she asked, "What kind of office are you running, Mr. Butters, that you do not even have coffee to offer a client?"

I guess I was wrong about her not sensing my presence.

"Second, cupboard over, Miss Wentworth… or shall I just call you Pamela."

Kicked back at my desk, I watched the shapely, future… depending on the courts… heiress, tackle the electric hot plate and coffee percolator like a professional.

She even hummed while she bustled about. I was hard pushed not to offer her a job as my secretary, given my previous one had hightailed it outta here without so much as a goodbye or a slap in the face.

Unless, of course, Pamela Wentworth's coffee killed me in the interim.

"So, Pamela, why in the heck did someone judge it necessary to teach you how to pick locks?" I asked when she joined me at my desk, setting a coffee cup in front of me, then taking the seat opposite.

If experience has taught me anything, it is to be vigilant of the person pouring the coffee, and to wait until they take the first sip.

At my question, mirth lurked in her eyes. "I learned that from my mama before papa sent her away. She thought I ought to learn a useful skill in case I found it necessary to escape an unpleasant situation."

My recent research still swirling around my brain, I recalled Pamela was sixth months shy of her tenth birthday when Old Man Wentworth evicted her mother. "You were a child," I blurted out, before common sense reasserted itself. "Apologies, but you were. What was your mother thinking?"

"That I am the daughter of a rich man, and not everyone can be trusted."

"Being prepared is one thing, breaking and entering, a whole other issue. What did you intend? To ransack it, maybe?"

"From the looks of the place, someone beat me to it," she scoffed, neatly sidestepping my accusation.

"It's the maid's day off."

"Sure." She smiled, taking another sip of her coffee.

Risking a mouthful, the taste surprised me. Despite only being able to afford cheap coffee with the rationing stamps, it seemed to possess a richer flavor, which caused my eyebrows to arch.

"Caramel. Found it in the back of your cupboard," she elaborated without being asked.

"Previous tenant must have forgotten it." I chuckled. "Don't remember ever buying any."

Placing my cup on the desk, I figured it was time to coax some answers from a woman who was supposed to be dead. "Tell me, did your mama teach you to kill, as well?"

I watched her eyes widen at the unexpected direction of our conversation. She spluttered, nearly choking on her coffee.

She set her cup down, her hand trembling. "W-what do you mean murder? My mama was a proud woman. Yeah, I cannot deny she had the blood of a bandida, and was a talented con-artist savvy enough to trick the old geezer who thought himself the smartest man in the room, but murder is not something she would condone."

"How do you account for the body they dredged up from the Bay? My sources say the victim, a woman who resembles you too closely to ignore, took a swan dive off of the Bridge near where the cops found your car. Are you saying that was a coincidence?"

I did not bother to mention the victim was strangled first. I was anxious to see whether the multi-faceted femme-fatale… alleged… would trip herself up by pointing out the missing piece of evidence.

She did not.

"Do I look capable of tossing someone off the Golden Gate Bridge?"

"That's like asking why you know how to pick a lock. Can you explain why your car and purse were found abandoned on the Bridge?"

"Because I wanted to make it look as though I had committed suicide, in order to find out who is trying to kill me."

"You expect me to believe, you came upon the scene inadvertently and, instead of reporting it, decided to use it your advantage? You do know how crazy that makes you sound? A trait, I believe, which negates any claim you have on the inheritance, and could see you in a padded cell. What do you mean *trying to kill you?*"

Pamela picked up her cup to take another sip of the aromatic brew, apparently in an attempt to calm her nerves, then without warning banged it down on the desk. I thought for sure she had shattered it

"I thought that statement was fairly self-explanatory," she snapped.

Her mercurial mood swings captivated me, but did not eliminate her from the list of suspects in the Dutchman's murder. In fact, they catapulted her all the way to the top.

Bristling like a scalded cat, Pamela gathered her things. "I thought you might be different. More fool me. Seems you're as incompetent as the damn cops in this corrupt town."

· · ·

I half-rose. "Whoa, hang on a minute. I came in on the second act of this play, how about catching me up from the start."

Pamela paused, considering her next move. Huffing a sigh, she resumed her seat. "No sense in wasting a good cup of coffee," she justified her change of heart.

I contemplated the wisdom of checking my crockery to make certain she had not stolen a couple of pieces to use on me during her next outburst.

Making herself comfortable, she began her tale. "For you to understand, we need to go back before my father's death."

I settled into my chair, presuming it was going to be a long story… surprisingly…

"Mama went to work for the Wentworths when papa's first wife was ill. Vanessa was at boarding school, and Mrs. Wentworth did not want her daughter to see her that way, which meant Vanessa was not there when her mother died. She was only a kid, poor thing." Pamela's features twisted with an empathy, I did not expect, given the state of their relationship and that this had happened before she was born.

She threw it off, and continued, "Papa did not cope well living alone in a large mansion, and it did not take long for him to find other distractions. Soon enough, the cute Mexican maid caught his eye. Before you knew it, the rich old man was expecting another child.

"Mama made sure others were aware of her condition, so he could neither deny paternity nor force her to get rid of me. I guess he was caught between a rock and a hard place, and basically threw in the towel. He turned over the running of the household to my mother, as if the two were married, which included managing Vanessa's school expenses.

"Somehow mama persuaded papa the school had

increased the fees, and she put the excess into an account only I could touch when I turned twenty-one.

"When he figured out the glitch in the records, to the tune of about fifty thousand dollars, he was furious. Funnily enough, I think he was more upset that mama had swindled him right under his nose than the embezzlement itself.

"He kicked her out but refused to let her take me. Something about protecting my soul from her evil influence. If he only knew the extent of what mama taught me while I was growing up," Pamela mused almost absently, "but I digress."

Her slightly sinister grin was not unnerving at all.

"I don't think he liked the idea of being alone. To be fair, he doted on me and never demanded I return the money. In fact, he kept adding to the account without telling me. Today, it's worth over a quarter of a million."

"Okay, now *I'm* confused," I replied. "Obviously, you have no need to battle for cash with Vanessa, so why are you fighting her in court?"

"She is trying to prove coercion on my part and that the private account should be included in the total amount."

"Where does this attempted murder come in?"

"About a week ago, I awoke to find a mountain of a man in my bedroom, trying to smother me with my pillow. Thankfully, I relied on another skill I learned as a child, one papa taught me. Self-defense.

"His greatest fear was that someone might try to kidnap me and hold me for ransom. He wanted to be sure, if I could not fight them off, I left enough scratches and bruises, they could be identified easily.

"I guess the thug didn't expect to lose handfuls of greasy hair or have his eyes gouged. Sadly, the room was dark, so I didn't get a good look at his face." She growled her aggravation.

"One last question." *In for a penny, in for a pound.* "I assume it was you looking for the Dutchman this morning, why?"

"I heard he specialized in forging legal documents, and before you ask how I knew, mama's side of the family are not saints either. I contacted my uncle who told me where to find him."

"Okay, I can accept that," I conceded, adding curiously. "Did you speak to him?"

"No. I don't know whether he was deliberately ignoring my knock or genuinely wasn't there."

CHAPTER SIX

While we were talking the sun had set and the room was shrouded in gloom. I switched on the desk lamp, remembering I was supposed to check in on Vanessa, a detail I was not ready to share with her younger sister. This was a game of truth and lies and, at this early stage, both stories sounded credible.

Who did I trust?

My gut told me Pamela was not being deceitful *but*, in light of what Vanessa had told me yesterday, it was incumbent on me to reserve my judgement.

Not for the first time, not even for the thousandth time, I wished Stella was here. Her ability to filter through the bullshit to reach the crux of the matter was unmatched.

I confess Pamela's sultry beauty was enchanting, and the last thing I needed was to get distracted, studiously ignoring the ribald laughter at the back of my brain telling me I was already sliding down a slippery slope.

Shrugging it off, I suggested we take break and resume our discussion the following afternoon. "I have a few leads I want to chase up. Hopefully, I'll have more to tell you tomorrow."

If Pamela discerned my prevarication, she gave no indication. She looked sad and lost. Kicking myself for being a glutton for punishment, I said. "Are you hungry? I know a quiet place close by where no one cares who you are and no questions are asked."

She lifted a troubled gaze and studied me, doubtless wondering whether I had an ulterior motive. I could have stared into her eyes forever.

Stop it Butters. Client and possible murderer. Get a grip.

I raised my palms. "Not trying to trick you. Just a gesture."

I watched her dither.

"The food is exceptional." I dangled the carrot.

Her shoulders slumped. "Okay, you win, but no funny business."

"Scout's honour." I saluted glad to hear a soft chuckle in response.

For the rest of the evening, I made a concerted effort to keep Pamela's mind off the drama stalking her. Over dinner, which she agreed was delicious, we talked about anything and everything else. It transpired, despite our drastically different backgrounds, we had similar views on many subjects.

Candid, intelligent, and witty, Pamela... in contrast with many of her peers... could hold her own on any given issue and, although her name opened doors, literally and figuratively, I was quick to realise she did not rely on goodwill, nor take it for granted.

It was obvious she relished a good debate, had no qualms about playing devil's advocate if the mood took her, and did not suffer fools gladly. A worthy foe, in fact, and I enjoyed our verbal fencing match, remarking that she would do well in politics.

"You have a silver tongue, Mr Butterfield." She grinned.

"Butters… since it appears were are working together."

"We are?" Pamela stared at me guilelessly and, to my shock, I felt my heart skip a beat. *Oh hell no.*

The longer I spent in her company the further under her spell, I fell.

Over the next few days, I tracked down snippets of information, gathered what negligible evidence I could, and kept my two clients abreast of what I had unearthed… very little.

The dance was exhausting and, trying to remember not to slip up and tell the wrong sister something meant for the other's ears only was giving me a headache… or possibly an ulcer.

I would have to be an idiot not to suppose each was trying to set up the other, or me. The problem being, the pair were so damn plausible, and it was becoming tantamount to not seeing the forest for the trees.

That said, I am a great believer in instinct and, without blowing my own trumpet, have become quite discerning over the years. Assume everyone is guilty until proven otherwise is a great starting point and my usual modus operandi. Cynical? Maybe but it has saved my life on more than one occasion.

Slowly whittling away at the evidence until, as one of my heroes, the great Sherlock Holmes, said, 'When you have eliminated the impossible, whatever remains however improbable must be the truth.'

Unfortunately, the improbable might also be unpalatable because, on top of everything else, my relationship with

Pamela was undergoing an almost indiscernible change, one I dared not acknowledge. Unprofessional at best, sleazy at worst.

Never mind that I was over a decade older, grew up on the wrong side of the tracks, and earned a living investigating people's misfortunes. Not the most attractive prospect for a beautiful young lady.

I would cross that bridge if I came to it.

"Jacob Butters, you are a walking cliche this morning," I muttered to myself as I climbed the stairs to my office intent on reviewing my notes.

To my relief, Vanessa and Esmerelda had reached a precarious truce, but the former was obviously exasperated at her enforced sequestration. A quick resolution would be better for all concerned or, I had no doubt, sparks would fly.

I knew Pamela had visited Van Dijk to whom, she claimed, she did not speak. Did I believe her? Was she also the sister who went to the morgue? The answers to those two questions were pivotal.

Identifying yourself as the body on the slab was perverse but, after listening to Pamela's side of the sorry tale — *if* she was the mysterious Joan Doe — the gesture had a bizarre logic.

Alternatively, if it was Vanessa, firstly, she had obviously already been to the morgue before she turned up at my door, with her tearful blue eyes and sob story and, secondly, she had played fast and loose with the truth at the coroner's office, which led me down a completely different and far more insidious track.

I could not discount any scenario, or any suspect at this juncture. I *did* want to yank my hair out.

Revisiting the Dutchman was crucial. I had no doubt he had spoken to either Vanessa or Pamela, possibly both... depending on who wanted what from the old forger... at some point. While their features marked them as sisters, one was blonde and one dark — enough to distinguish who had sought his services.

Glancing at the clock I noticed it was coming up to lunchtime, and weighed up whether it was worth the drive, knowing I had no choice. "Come on, Butters do your job." Refusing to acknowledge that my reticence related to a welter of emotions, I scarcely recognized and would never be reciprocated. We belonged to different worlds.

Squaring my shoulders — as a general rule, I am not one for introspection — I hopped into the DeSoto and retraced my route to The Embarcadero.

It was a glorious day. Any early morning fog, for which our fair city is famous, had evaporated under the dazzling summer sunshine. Awaiting the tide, a proud array of ships floated like huge grey leviathans on the glittering water of the Bay. It was an impressive spectacle.

The blare from the horn of an oncoming car, snapped my attention back to the road. Swerving at the last minute, I traded paint with a dark blue Chevrolet convertible charging straight towards me. It was only my skillful driving which prevented me from becoming its hood ornament.

Avoiding the deep blue sea was another question.

Slamming on the brakes, I stopped inches short of tipping into the drink.

Letting my nerves settle for a moment, I drove on and parked near the dilapidated wooden shanty on the last pier, which looked as though it expected to be swallowed by the Bay.

Sadly, its grave was not to be watery.

CHAPTER SEVEN

Before I had the chance to rap a knuckle on Van Dijk's door, never mind speak to the old man, I questioned whether the whole world had suffered a catastrophic eruption, or whether that distant war had landed on our shores without warning

Three strides from my car, I was launched into the air and flung backwards, crashing into the uncompromising metal of the DeSoto's front fender before slithering to the ground in a crumpled heap.

Stunned, and momentarily paralyzed, I struggled into a sitting position, flexing my limbs, praying they were still attached. Trying to shake the ringing from my ears, I forced my trembling body to do my bidding, and twisted in the direction of the blast.

The Shack.

Adrenaline coursing through my veins, and acting on instinct, I did the last thing *anyone* should do.

Rushing to the front door, I hurled myself against it. As the weathered wood gave way, a fireball whooshed out stealing the air from my lungs.

Certain I had been cauterized — I could smell my singed hair, and my eyes stung — I hacked a cough to expel the gases, yanked my handkerchief from my pocket, covered my mouth and nose, and charged through the inferno.

On the floor lay Levi Van Dijk.

The detonation had catapulted the old printing press from its precarious perch to its new resting place on the Dutchman's chest. Stooping over the old man, I took in his charred face and hands. Blood oozed from his mouth, and I registered, even with my compromised hearing, that his breathing was labored.

While this was bad, very bad, there were other wounds... bruising and lacerations which could not possibly be the result of the machine landing on him. To my reasonably expert eye, he had been beaten up. Probably a couple of days ago.

Probably following your visit, a snarky voice hissed at the back of my mind. I refused to give the notion house room and focused on Van Dijk.

Lack of medical training aside, I surmised, at the very minimum, he had suffered several broken ribs which had punctured his lungs.

Mindful the proprietor was a victim here and unlikely to destroy his own, extremely profitable, if not entirely legal, business, I speculated that the explosion was caused by some kind of crude, time-delayed bomb, set to ignite the sickening sweet smelling, and highly flammable chemical, benzene. An element the Dutchman used to create his colored dyes.

This allowed the perpetrator to flee the scene; the image of a speeding blue car swam across my vision. The intensity of the blaze would almost certainly destroy any evidence of whatever device was used, the cause ascribed to an old man being careless with his compounds.

By sheer luck, I had not reached the shack when it went up but, if I did not move my ass, I might well become its next victim.

Scooping Van Dijk from the floor, I carried him out of the building and laid him on the gravel gently. Through a paroxysm of coughing, he tried to speak. I bent over him until my ear was close to his lips.

His final words were not a confession I could take to Mazzetti, just a rasped, "Wentwo…"

He expired on a gruesome hiss of blood escaping his lungs, even as I shook him, demanding, "Which one?"

The thunderous *whump*, along with the billowing black plume from the combination of old wood and flammable materials acted like a beacon. Curiosity seekers from the docks and surrounding ships congregated around the burning shack and the dead man sprawled alongside my car.

The wail of sirens from the San Francisco Fire Department signaled their arrival, as well as that of the South Station Detectives.

Flanked by various city vehicles, it was not long before I noticed Captain Mazzetti standing next to me, watching the firemen struggling to extinguish the flames. His expression of disgust was not directed at the losing battle they were fighting.

Half-jokingly, I asked, "Isn't a Waterfront arson a little beneath you?" My attempt at humor fell on deafer ears than mine.

"Christ, Butters, is there anywhere you don't go where somebody doesn't end up dead?"

"Not sure, but then I haven't been everywhere yet," I parried mildly.

Refusing to look at me, he groused, "Convince me the

Arson boys aren't gonna find your fingerprints all over in there when they start looking."

"Given the state of the place, I doubt they'll be able to find anything."

"In that case, you can save me the trouble and confess now."

"To what?" I leaned against the fender trying, with limited success, to stop coughing.

"Killing the Dutchman."

"*What*? Why would I kill him?" I was thunderstruck by his wholly unjustified accusation.

"How the hell should I know? Maybe the two of you were scamming old ladies out of their life savings with phoney stocks, and he stiffed you on your cut. Anyway, the Hotline got an anonymous tip reporting a murder happening here, and you fit the description of the perp."

"Hang on, let me get this straight," I countered incredulously. "I was in the process of killing Van Dijk and setting his place on fire, stop me when you catch the irony, only to smash down his door... risking my own life, mind you... *to save him?*"

"You might have let him cook long enough to figure he'd die out here, so you could cover your ass."

"Oh, for crying out loud, Mazzetti, not even you are obtuse enough to believe a story like that."

"Then tell me why you're here?"

"I heard some dame was looking for the Dutchman and, given his skills, my interest was piqued."

"And?"

"And nothing. The place went boom. I'm guessing it was an incendiary device left by someone who does not like loose ends."

"Do you think it could be the same mystery woman who showed up at the morgue?" Mazzetti ruminated.

"I have no idea. I wasn't the one who saw her, but if you care to check Levi's body, someone had used him for boxing practice recently, so…" I left that dangling. After his idiotic allegation, I was *not* about to do the good captain's job for him.

"I'm sure the coroner will be thorough. Oh, and while we're on the topic of the City Morgue, don't let me catch you bothering Hamilton again. He works for us, not you."

"Feel better now you've reprimanded me, Dad?"

"Hardly," Mazzetti barked, then flicked a reproving hand at the damage to my car from the earlier near collision. "Learn to drive."

"Sure, sure. Anything else? Like I need to get a better class of friends and not smoke?" Needling my old partner might not be sensible, but he had ruffled my feathers, and it was better than smacking the stupid out of him.

"No, get out of my sight, Butterfield until I have the time and energy to take a statement from you."

He paused a moment, adding in his *I am a serious policeman tone*, "Don't even think about skipping town."

"As if the government is granting unnecessary travel during wartime," I retorted.

"See you stay put." Mazzetti fixed me with a glare, then wandered to the smoldering remains of the shack.

CHAPTER EIGHT

From the Wharf, I detoured past my office. I could not turn up at my landlady's apartment smelling like a barbecue, meaning a thorough scrub was in order, glad I kept a change of clothes there for emergencies. Not convinced I would ever rid myself of the stench, I had to try.

While I drove, I attempted to piece together who in the name of Dashiell Hammett might be sizing me up for this particularly uncomfortable frame. Questions were piling up, the answers to which Miss Vanessa Wentworth alone was likely to have.

Oh sure, I had my fair share of cheating husbands who might well want to exact their revenge… along with any number of Waterfront riffraff from my days on the police force.

Let's not forget a jilted lover or two. *Although, they would probably prefer to kill me themselves as opposed to trusting it to a third party.*

For a moment, Stella Fitzhugh's face splashed across my brain like an Academy Award winning picture on the silver screen.

No, I banished the image. The last I saw of her was from the Coast Line platform at the Southern Pacific Depot as she ended our relationship through the window of a train bound for Las Vegas, in company with one of the worst mobsters to whom she could cozy up… Carmine *aka Red,* Russo.

All because of my lack of attention.

Preferring not to wallow in self-pity, I adjusted my focus. An unpleasant thought struck me.

I let it take shape, ice slinking down my spine.

Could the culprit be Louis Mazzetti? I discounted it almost immediately. Since my less than auspicious departure from the force… all his fault… Lou's guilty conscience had worked in my favour and, his hasty assumptions aside, I believed we had brokered a tacit, if guarded, understanding.

That my former partner had chosen to be a dirty cop still left a nasty taste in my mouth although, I could not deny he had, of late, cleaned his act up… somewhat… and become a reasonably reliable source.

The thought of clueing in the captain about the Chevy which had aimed to make me shark bait tickled my fancy for about thirty seconds, to the point of filing an official complaint for Reckless Driving, or Attempted Murder, whichever would get a rise from Mazzetti.

Without a license plate number my description would match at least ten percent of vehicles in the Greater San Francisco Metropolitan Area.

By the time I arrived at the corner of 22nd and Sanchez, I was no longer pinning the blame on anyone else, convinced I was trying to frame myself.

To my everlasting astonishment, Pamela was sitting in the chair exactly as she had the day we met. Briefly, I contemplated the possibility this whole debacle was a figment of a lurid dream and I was about to wake up.

The welcome aroma of freshly brewed coffee crushed the hope.

"What brings you here?" I ventured, my voice a raspy croak, too tired to take her to task on her method of entry.

"I thought… hoped…" she started, stopped then blushed. My eyes widened. *Pamela Wentworth irresolute… interesting.* "I wondered whether you had any news." she finished in a rush.

Her nose crinkled as she registered my dishevelled appearance and pungent perfume. "Ewww… what happened?"

"I thought you might be able to tell me?"

"What?" her shock was genuine, of that I had no doubt.

"I was nearly killed. Down at the wharf." I did not elaborate, but skewered her with watchful eyes.

"Butters, Jacob… no. How? Why?" Her hand fluttered to her throat and she blanched. I confess, I was gratified by her reaction, and spontaneous use of my given name, but could not let emotion get in the way of the truth.

Taking a sip of the coffee she had just poured me, I said baldly, "You know the Dutchman is dead?"

"What?" she gawked, her eyes on stalks. Pamela was either an Oscar winning actress or she was sincerely flabbergasted.

"I was on my way to talk to him. Was within feet of the shack."

"I had nothing to do with the fire," she defended hotly.

"How did you know there was a fire? I didn't mention how he died."

"I may not have a Private Investigator's License but, unless you stand downwind from random conflagrations on a regular basis, it's clear you've been near burning chemicals recently," she countered her eyes glinting. "Never mind that you look like you challenged a bonfire to a brawl and lost."

"Did you kill him?" I asked flatly.

"Why in God's name would I do something so stupid? I needed to find out whether he had drafted the second will."

"You mean the one stating that if you were declared *unstable*, you'd lose everything?" I queried. "Yes, faking your death does foster an inclination to believe you're…" remembering the bewildered expression on the Dutchman as he tried to comprehend which of the two sisters had taken his life and why, "…insane."

"If he was involved with Vanessa, it was up to me to get him into the courtroom to prove my sister is trying to chisel me out of what is rightfully mine. I was nowhere near the docks." she argued. "If you bothered to use your eyes, you'll see I've been here, waiting for you."

I glanced around the office. It was spotless. All the paperwork had been, I assume, filed. The desk was polished, the floor swept and mopped, the kitchenette scrubbed within an inch of its life.

Even I had to concede her handiwork would take longer than five minutes, more like five hours.

"Yeah, this B&E is becoming a habit and, I repeat… insane. Your stunts could cost you your inheritance."

"Only if they prove the body they pulled out of the water is me… which, as you and I know, is impossible."

I bit my lip at the devilish twinkle in her eye, she did *not* need encouraging, and grumbled, "Still a crazy stunt. One last question. What do you want me to do about all of this?"

"I want you to make sure I don't end up in the Bay for real and find out who is hell-bent on putting me there."

"Okay," I capitulated, "but before we deal with that not so minor problem, there's something I have to tell you."

. . .

During the short drive to my apartment, and praying my intuition was firing on all cylinders, I gave Pamela chapter and verse, from the moment Vanessa sashayed into my office.

I could not shed the impression the whole thing was a set up; that Vanessa had sought me out deliberately, either as a witness or a fall-guy. No definitive proof, yet, but I did not figure the elder Wentworth sister to be a criminal master-mind extraordinaire, more a spoilt, jealous sibling who did not want to share, and had allowed resentment to rule her judgement.

She would make a mistake, eventually. Whether Pamela and I survived until she did was another matter entirely.

Listening intently as I talked, Pamela, rather than blow her top at my lack of faith in her veracity — a good thing, one explosion a day was all I could handle — asked pertinent questions and, by the time I snagged a parking space right outside my building, we were in accord.

I sensed the subtle shift between us was settling into something more tangible but, employing sheer effort of will, I squashed the tiny glimmer of hope. Stella Fitzhugh might think she could fall in love in a week. I was not that naive.

I helped Pamela from the car… yes, I can be quite the gent when circumstance dictates.

She paused, squeezing my hand briefly.

I met her gaze and, as we shared a smile, she inclined her head ever-so slightly.

In that moment, something clicked, and I knew. No words needed.

Dammit, my timing was shot to hell. Romance would have to take a back seat for now.

Professionalism took over and we hurried to my landla-dy's cluttered abode.

CHAPTER NINE

I tried slow my racing thoughts, sorely tempted, despite my feelings for Pamela, to create my own judicial precedent by locking the two wildcats in the same room without food or water.

Leave them to fight it out... err *discuss*... the situation until they agreed on a mutually beneficial solution to the legal chaos, without killing each other in the process.

Regrettably, fate had other plans.

From within Esmerelda's first-floor apartment, I heard the news headlines blaring from a radio.

I pounded on the door and waited but no one answered. A surreptitious twist of the knob confirmed it was locked.

A tap on the shoulder. I turned to be met with a disgusted eye roll and a thumb jerking to the right for me to get out of the way.

Pamela pulled a bobby pin from under her felt pillbox hat. "Now you know why these come in handy."

My bruised ego aside, I felt moved to point out, a trifle testily, "I could have done that had you given me a minute."

The lock yielded under her skilled touch. She straightened up and ran her index finger along my jaw, "Of that, I have no doubt."

I suppressed the urge to kiss her senseless… a delight that would have to wait… drew my gun, something which was becoming a regular event today, and entered the old lady's apartment. The place looked even worse than my place upstairs. Furniture was overturned and it appeared a life-or-death struggle had taken place.

Facing away from the door, Esmeralda Harper was bound to one of the kitchen chairs. For a split, and gut-wrenching, second, I questioned whether she was still alive. Relief swamped me when I stepped closer, and saw her jerk, realizing whoever had tied her to the chair had also blindfolded her.

"Who's there," she bellowed. "Take me on in a fair fight this time and I'll beat your ass."

Spinning her chair around, I was grateful her legs had been secured, because she was desperately trying to kick out, and the last thing I needed was a foot to the groin.

I yanked the blindfold down. "Miss Harper, it's me Butterfield."

That news seemed to trigger an even greater fury.

"Goddamnit, Butterfield, what did you get me into?" she snarled.

I signaled to Pamela to turn off the radio. Trying to discuss anything over the din was pointless.

"What happened?" I asked when blessed peace enveloped the room.

"Some goon banged on the door, said he was a cop. I checked through the peephole, and he looked like one. I'd barely turned the key when he shouldered the door into me so hard I almost fell over. I tried to fight back…" she seemed ashamed he had got the better of her, "…but the bastard socked me in the jaw."

The livid bruise on her chin verified her struggle.

"What kinda man hits a woman?" she groused rhetorically. "If I was ten years younger, he wouldn't have got the chance."

Silence fell. It ought to have been welcome, but the unnatural hush gnawed at me.

Light dawned.

"Esmeralda, where's Vanessa?"

"How the hell should I know?" the old lady huffed. "I've been stuck in this chair for hours. He musta taken her. Untie me, Butters," she bleated. "You owe me *four* bottles of rum for my troubles."

I glanced at Pamela, who was as white as a ghost, "Jacob, d-do you think it could be the same man?"

It made sense that, regardless of their animosity, the half-sisters were still blood, and Pamela was concerned for Vanessa's safety.

"That would be my guess," I said as, using a lethal-looking pair of scissors procured from Esmerelda's silverware drawer, I released my landlady from her bonds.

I looked around, something did not feel right. I mean, yeah, if old man Wentworth had taught his younger daughter self-defense, it stood to reason his elder daughter had received the same instruction.

The room was *too* tossed.

In my humble opinion, had Joe Louis and Max Schmeling gone fifteen rounds in here, they would not have caused this much damage.

Freed, the elderly woman bolted out of the chair and elbowed her way past me to inspect her apartment. "Jacob Butterfield," she threatened as she righted her furniture, "if I find anything broken, it's coming out of your security deposit."

At the state of the place, I might as well kiss that money goodbye.

Pamela saved the day. "Miss Harper, I am afraid my sister and I are responsible for this unprovoked attack on you and your home. I shall ensure you are reimbursed for any damage."

My landlady forced a smile. "That is sweet of you, dear. I'm sure everything will be fine… but I'll let you know."

I pictured a new parlor suite in the old lady's future, but that was between the two of them.

We left Esmerelda to draw up the bill.

In the hallway, the door shut behind us, Pamela whispered forlornly, "What do we do now? Where do you think he took her?"

At the sight of tears welling in her eyes, I bit the inside of my cheek, wanting to slap Miss Vanessa Wentworth into next year for her atrocious behaviour.

"Do you honestly believe she was kidnapped?" I knew accepting her sister was the brains behind this debacle and not acting under duress was a bitter pill to swallow, but the truth can be ugly.

She stared at me for long moments, and I could almost hear the gears grinding in her brain. "I'd prefer that over the alternative," she confessed. "She's my sister."

"I know, but we have to face facts." I instilled a brisk note into my voice. I didn't want to be cruel, but I needed gutsy, defiant Pamela, not her subdued shadow.

"Ok, we have two choices," I started not liking either option. "We can turn this over to San Francisco's finest and watch them screw everything up, or we can go to your place."

"My place? Why would going to my apartment help?" Her brow creased in confusion.

"I'm not thinking of your apartment, more like the mansion. I have a feeling, if this is a legitimate kidnap, you'll hear from him shortly. That is, if he hasn't called already."

"Why would anybody contact me? I'm supposed to be dead, remember."

"Presumably, someone knows that's not true."

Looping my arm through hers, I escorted her to my coupe. Pamela leaned against me for support, the drama taking its toll.

After assisting her into the front seat of the DeSoto, I got behind the wheel, switched on the ignition, and pointed the car toward Pacific Heights.

I was going to get an earful from Mazzetti for not checking in and apprising him of my suspicions. Time was of the essence and I could not afford any delay while he determined whether I was right.

Even though I hoped I was wrong.

Pamela did not speak as we crossed the city, her attention fixed on the view outside the window.

Following her directions, I turned into a leafy lane, then through a pair of monumental, and ridiculously elaborate, wrought-iron gates which stood open — something Pamela commented on with a frown — and followed the winding drive, coming to a halt on the circular frontage which surrounded a fountain. *Wow.*

Hopping out, I opened her door with all the formality of a chauffeur, waited for her to alight, then escorted her to the front door. Ushering her inside, I noticed that not only had she fallen quiet, but also, the entire house was blanketed in silence.

"Is any of the help here?" I ventured in low tones.

"No, until we settled everything, Vanessa and I agreed not to waste money unnecessarily."

Unaccountably, the fact the house was empty made me sigh. "Why don't you find us something to eat," I suggested, "and I'll put the car in the garage. No sense in advertising our presence."

Pamela shrugged listlessly. "The garage is around the side. Just come in through the domestic entrance and meet me in the kitchen."

Swallowing an irreverent grin at her terminology and assuming this meant the back door, I nodded. "Okay. Oh, and promise me, if the phone rings, you will not answer it until I'm with you."

"Whatever," was her last word as she walked towards a dim corridor at the far side of the atrium.

Retracing my steps, I drove the car around the grand mansion, agog at the sheer scale of the place, which reminded me of the châteaux I saw during the war — rambling monstrosities owned by French aristocrats — and wondered how much the old man had squandered on his residence.

The garage was closed. Killing the engine, I climbed out, approached the doors, and peeked through the windows.

What I saw made my blood run cold. The same late model, dark blue Chevrolet convertible which had scraped me this morning, was parked neatly at the right-hand side.

CHAPTER TEN

S wiveling, I looked for and spotted the back door. Pulling my revolver from its holster, I charged across the gravel, my hand gripping the knob and yanking before my feet landed on the top step. Locked, the door did not budge, and my momentum toppled me backwards.

Clearly, security was paramount. Considering the wealth of the successive owners, I supposed that was fair enough, but annoying nonetheless. Never happened like this in the books... or the movies. How can the hero save the day if thwarted by a locked door?

Without a second's thought, and ruining the element of surprise, I fired two quick slugs into the handle, then kicked the door with such force, the frame splintered.

There was no sign of Pamela. I crossed the kitchen, and paused to listen at the baize door... yes, an actual baize door... leading to the rest of the house, alert to the slightest noise.

A heavy and rhythmic stomp on a tiled floor indicated a large individual, almost certainly the gorilla who tried to kill Pamela and assaulted my landlady, was approaching. Hoping to time it right, I waited until I estimated he was on the other side, and barrelled into the door as hard as I could.

A solid **thud**, reverberated through the paneling, but the accompanying grunt led me to believe I had probably stunned rather than incapacitated him.

Doubtless being more brawn than brain is preferable when someone tries to render you insensible with a solid oak door.

A guttural growl reached me, and the image of a bear waking from hibernation prompted me to move before his momentary daze wore off.

Too late.

The door did not even swing back before it was torn open. Massive paws grabbed me by the lapels of my check-ered sports coat and pitched me into the dining room as though I weighed no more than a ragdoll.

Like a pinball, I slid along the polished table, bouncing off a couple of the elegant chairs, before tumbling headlong onto the floor.

Winded, I lay under the table, hearing him barrelling towards me. Yanking my snub nose from my ankle holster, I fired two bullets into my attacker's lower leg, bringing him to his knees.

This handed me the opportunity to squeeze off one more shot, which hit him square in the torso. Clutching his chest, the thug toppled onto his side. I didn't bother to check his vitals.

That heavy pall of silence which had enveloped the edifice on our arrival was well and truly shattered. Any racket caused my encounter with the grizzly, paled in comparison with the screaming emanating from elsewhere in the house.

Leaping to my feet, I tried to pin-point the origin, but the extensive interior made it impossible.

Thankfully, Fate was in a benevolent mood.

At the far side of the cavernous entrance hall, a set of double doors stood open. As I crept closer the shouting got louder. Becoming one with the door jamb, I peered around to see it was a study, in the middle of which stood the sisters, shrieking at each other like banshees.

"You never loved father. You are no better than that whore of a woman who bore you, using him for his money," Vanessa bellowed at her sister, incandescent with rage.

Pamela snorted derisively. "How *dare* you question my devotion to papa. You weren't even there, only bothering to turn up and smile sweetly when you wanted money. You have no idea how hard it was to keep him going after he sent mama away and you had all but abandoned him. The poor man had lost the will to live. Somebody needed to take care of him."

While the two were evenly matched in passion and intensity, the .32 automatic Vanessa was clutching in her hand, put Pamela at a definite disadvantage.

Vanessa must have spotted me from the corner of her eye because, abruptly, her features went from contorted with fury to coolly composed. She altered the angle of her body slightly. "Ah, Mr. Butterfield, your arrival is most fortuitous. Saves me the trouble of hunting you down. Please drop your revolver and take a seat by the fireplace.

"I daresay you might appreciate a front row seat when my darling Pamela murders you, after which, utterly distraught, she kills herself… for real this time." In contrast with the look she sent Pamela, which dripped with venom, her inflexion was light and airy, almost sing-song.

Disturbing does not begin to describe it. Vanessa Wentworth made fairy tale villains look like the angelic host.

"I do not like loose ends, and this is easier than trying to persuade some doctor, in light of the faked suicide and spectacularly irrational behaviour, to commit Pamela to a cozy psychiatric ward for the duration. Neither do I want the expense."

Easier? Mentally, I palmed my forehead. I knew which sibling needed committing and it was *not* the younger one. With increasing rapidity, dread coiling in my gut, I invented and discarded scenarios where we escaped unscathed. None were even vaguely feasible, but it helped focus my mind.

"Vanessa," I could see the effort it took for Pamela to soften her tone. "I told you. I don't want the money. I'm happy with what's in my account."

"Oh, Pammy, darling Pammy," Vanessa cooed with feigned warmth. "I know, as your older sister, I ought to feel a certain obligation, but this is less a matter of me worrying about your financial stability…" her voice hardened, "…and more about whether you might resort to dabbling in a little blackmail?"

Keenly aware their argument could flare up again, and unsure whether Vanessa's goon, if not dead, was suitably immobilized, I reckoned now was as good as any time to distract her. "Tell me, Vanessa, how did you know Pamela had not killed herself?"

To my relief, Vanessa seemed willing, nay eager to spill the beans. It's always useful to stroke to ego of the emotionally unstable, and where is the reward if the perpetrator is the only one who knows how well the murder was planned?

"Oh, Butters," she gloated. "I know my sister all too well. She is too much of a coward to try a stunt so bold. Although, I'm prepared to afford her some credit for taking advantage of that poor girl's suicide to stage her own death. Sheer dumb luck. What are the chances somebody jumped from the bridge on the same night?"

"That doesn't explain how you knew for sure," I pressed.

"Gracious, you're a stickler for details. It was that courteous Captain Mazzetti. He contacted Walter — you know, the man you murdered in cold blood, who was only trying to protect me — and asked him to take me to the city morgue to identify the poor girl. I was over the moon to discover the truth, which I kept to myself."

"If you knew she was alive, why attack my landlady?" I could not mask my anger, and my mind whirled. Vanessa's intention was clear. Leaving a string of bodies in her wake, she would get off scot free, especially when her explanation of events, delivered with the perfect blend of shock and distress, ensured all the blame landed squarely at my feet. Difficult for the dead to repudiate an accusation with… you know… facts.

"Had to make you think the worst, didn't I? Took ya no time to scurry over here. Besides, have you ever spent time with that old bat? Nightmare. Between her screeching and the radio blaring, my eardrums all but ruptured."

"What about the Dutchman?" Running out of stalling tactics, I was interested to note, now Vanessa had turned to face me, Pamela was inching closer to the desk. I could not see what she was after.

"You can't blame me for that. The old fool brought it on himself. He couldn't be trusted to keep his mouth shut about the wills, and allowed greed to trump common sense, daring to demand a bigger cut. Besides, I was not responsible for the explosion. I had an alibi remember?" She sent me a sly smile.

Appalled and fascinated at how blithely she dismissed the taking of a life… four if I was counting… and, given the number included me, I was… to satisfy her agenda, I almost felt sorry for Walter. He was as much a dupe as the rest of us.

"If you cannot come up with another ruse to delay your demise, Mr. Butterfield," Vanessa's lip curled sardonically and she aimed the gun at me, "I must bid you adieu."

Before she could pull the trigger, I caught the glint of silver and a lethal-looking object plunged into Vanessa's shoulder. Howling in pain, the gun flew out of her hand to land on the floor at my feet.

In a flash, I grabbed it and leveled it at the would-be killer who was sobbing piteously while struggling to wrest an ornate letter opener from her back. My, reasonable I thought, suggestion she leave it until she got to a hospital, in case she bled out, was met with a malevolent glare.

Pamela looked inordinately pleased with herself, evoking the proverbial cat who ate the canary — an extraordinarily rich cat.

I swear she called her sister a *bitch* but, with all the screaming who could tell.

POSTSCRIPT

When the San Francisco Police Department arrived at the opulent Pacific Heights mansion, Captain Louis Mazzetti took charge… and the credit for solving the murder of Levi Van Dijk, aka the Dutchman.

It helped that he was the one to find the bloody tire iron in the trunk of the convertible, covered with Walter's fingerprints.

As for Walter Berger, he survived my marksmanship and is recovering in the San Quentin Prison medical facility. Mazzetti estimates he should be completely healed in time for his date with the gas chamber next spring.

His accomplice, the former heiress Vanessa Wentworth avoided the same fate, thanks to a plea for clemency from Pamela. She no longer has to worry about the state of her finances because, for the term of her natural life, she will be taken care of by the California Institution for Women at Tehachapi.

On the topic of Pamela Wentworth, she is now a very wealthy woman who has, inexplicably, developed a penchant for making me coffee every day. Turns out, she is not in the slightest fazed by the difference in our ages… apparently, it makes me worldly and distinguished. I can live with that!

Oh, and if you are in need of a gumshoe, I recommend continuing to thumb through the yellow pages. The fourth-floor office on 22nd and Sanchez, formerly the home of the Butterfield Detective Agency, is closed for business.

These days, yours truly is often featured in the tabloids, escorting the beautiful Pamela Wentworth to glittering events, and acting as her muscle. It's a tough gig, but I'm not complaining.

If, by chance, you happen across a picture of us dressed in white, make sure to send all wedding gifts to Mr. and Mrs. Jacob Butterfield, Wentworth Mansion, Pacific Heights. The happy couple…

The dissonant chime of the telephone startled me out of my reverie.

Typical… interrupted by the bell.

Please excuse me for a moment.

"Hello, Butterfield residence."

"Jacob, thank God, I found you," It was the anxious voice of Hamilton Washington. "There's been another murder by strangulation, and the brass won't believe there's a connection to that Jane Doe. I need to call in one of my markers and get your—"

"I'm sorry, Hamilton, but the Butterfield Detective Agency is terminated. Might I recommend—"

"Who is it, dear? A friend in need?"

I turned to see my gorgeous wife already getting her hat and gloves.

"Yes," Hamilton's yell floated out of the handset.

Pamela reached my side and stroked slender fingers along my arm. "Jacob, dear Jacob, we cannot let down a friend. That is simply unkind and uncalled for. What sort of private detective are you?"

"I assumed a retired one," I tried to deflect to no avail. "Darling…"

Snatching the phone from my hand, Pamela announced with un-heiress-like glee, "Whoever this is, we will be right over."

As I was saying, the happy couple will be God knows where.

THE MOBSTER'S MOLL

Butters P.I

——————

CHAPTER ONE

——————

1947 - San Francisco

The shrill peal of several telephones ruptured the comfortable hush of the mansion: their, not so melodious, jingles reverberating off tastefully papered walls and down spacious hallways.

Every last one went unanswered.

It was July 4th, 1947. My wife and I were relaxing by our newly installed pool… some distance from the main house… and our wonderful, all be they long suffering, staff were enjoying a welcome day off to mark the country's independence.

Currently, swimming laps, I was savoring the tranquility, while Pamela, pretending to read the glossy magazine on her knee watched me over the top of her large sunglasses. I admit, being the object of her admiration boosted my ego and spurred me to continue cutting through the crystal clear water.

I was determined that, despite me celebrating my forty-seventh birthday recently, my darling wife who is twelve years my junior, would not find my physical prowess lacking.

I could hear her gloating gleefully, *See, you big lug, refusing to let you retire to become an idle... and, doubtlessly, podgy... bum was the best wedding present I gave you.*

As I turned at the end of the pool, I noticed her glancing at the martini shaker on the little round table beside her, even from several feet away, I could tell it was empty and, in the heat of the summer afternoon, the glasses had lost their inviting frostiness.

Shamelessly, she is my wife after all, I stared at Pamela's slender figure as, with efficiency of movement, she balanced everything on the silver tray and sashayed across the lush lawns to the house.

Five years of marriage, and we still behaved like loved-up fools. As a man who thought the notion of a happily ever after should be consigned to fairy tales, I finally understood the phrase *wedded bliss*. I know, I know... coming from a jaded ex-police officer turned private detective, that sounds sappy and, I would not change it for the world.

I grinned to myself. Pamela knew she had caught my eye and was teasing me. Never one to turn down such a blatant offer, I climbed out of the pool, grabbed the towel I had dropped on the lounger, and dried myself off.

When Pamela opened the French doors leading to my office, I heard the faint chime of the telephone, and groaned under my breath. *Who on earth is bothering us today?* I scoured my brain trying to recall whether I had forgotten something important, but came up blank.

She disappeared inside, and I pictured her rolling her eyes at the paperwork and books littering my desk, then felt my face scrunch up in a dismayed grimace, helpless to prevent a pile of documents toppling off when she slid the tray onto the surface.

This is why I designated my study a no go zone, to avoid the possibility of anyone upsetting my system, however inadvertently. I know Pamela, who claims it is a miracle I can find anything, is desperate to tidy up the disaster…her words, but I can put my hands on whatever I need at a moment's notice.

Pamela's cheerful, "Butterfield residence," rang out, but I was not close enough to identify the caller, all I could hear was a tinny response.

I was at the door when, in a puzzled voice my wife asked, "I apologize. We did not expect to be disturbed on this beautiful *holiday*," she emphasized the last word, but obviously did not feel obliged to justify why we had not answered immediately.

The caller spoke and, at Pamela's, "Uh, yes, but he is outside," my heart sank. *Not today.*

Something made Pamela pull the handset away from her ear and stare at it in confusion. I could almost see the cogs whirring in her brain. My instinct told me this was not someone calling to invite us to an impromptu Independence Day party. Almost at the door, I put a spurt on.

Pamela put the phone back against her ear. "I'm sorry, who is this?"

Whatever the caller said shocked Pamela so much, she sagged against the desk, and her hip jolted the tray. The martini shaker, wedged precariously among the glasses, teetered and tumbled off in a slow arc, splintering into myriad glittering, jagged pieces when it hit the oak floor.

I burst into the office just in time to see the shaker explode, and all color leach from Pamela's face. What, under any other circumstances, would have elicited a volley of curses, went unnoticed.

Alarmed, I was at her side in a flash, avoiding the shards

of glass. Trying to snap her out of her shock, I grasped her upper arms and shook her gently. "Pammie, what is it?"

"The call is for you, *Detective* Butterfield. Your ex," Pamela's tone was as devoid of emotion as were her features of her customary smile. "Apparently, she needs help and the only person in the whole damn world she could think of contacting is you." The anger simmering beneath her tones was unmistakable.

"Stella Fitzhugh?" For a moment, I gawked stupidly between the telephone and Pamela's furious face.

I stretched around her to take the handset, but she slammed it on the desk. The paper and debris strewn about managing to buffer the force somewhat, but Stella surely must have heard it. Berating me in outraged silence, my wife spun on her shapely legs and stormed out.

I heard her heels clicking on the marble stairs, and winced at the rattle of our bedroom door being shut with extreme force.

I grabbed the handset before it joined the martini shaker on the floor, and ventured, not quite able to mask my incredulity, "Stella? Is it really you? After all this time?"

"Listen, Jake, this is anything but a cordial phone call. I've been arrested for murder. You're the only one I could think of calling for help."

"Wait, are you back in San Francisco? You should have called Lou Mazzetti fir—"

"Would you shut up and listen? I am still in Las Vegas. I'm being charged with Red's murder."

"Probably the smartest thing you've done in the last seven years," I muttered loud enough for her to hear.

"Don't be a child, Butters," I was all too familiar with her condescension. "No, I did not shoot him, but the idiots here refuse to believe me. Not helped by the fact, the DA is running for governor and, presumably, hanging my husband's murder on me guarantees him the governor's mansion. Look, I'm running out of time for this call. Just get here quickly, and put that license *I* organized to good use."

"You know it's only valid in California," my protest was lost to a dial tone, as the call disconnected.

Replacing the handset on the cradle, I looked at the mess on the floor while considering whether I dare travel east.

Concluding I could, quite easily, leave Stella in the lurch, I also elected to leave the glass where it lay and let the staff earn their keep. Yes, it would be tomorrow but, did I care? Not a single jot.

Self-destruction being my middle name, and hating being on the outs with Pamela, I ran upstairs to our room.

Aware my darling wife had, unceremoniously, banged the door shut, I was surprised to find it unlocked. Peering around, I was greeted with the sight of two small suitcases on the bed, an assortment of Pamela's clothes were stuffed into one and she was pulling more from the closet.

Afraid to approach her, I asked sheepishly, "Can we talk first?"

"No… nor do I feel like it. So, button it, and start packing."

"Wait, are you kicking me out?"

"For Chrissakes, Jacob, do you, for one second, imagine I have any intention of letting you go to Vegas to see *that woman* by yourself?"

RORI BLEU

With a smattering of riverboat pirates and royalty in her
heritage, Rori Bleu's childhood reflected her past.
An interest in fairy tales, myth and legend were as important
as spirited discussions around politics and current affairs —
although some might argue they are one and the same!

A fascination, sparked by listening to Grimm's Fairy Tales at
her grandmother's knee, not only encouraged Rori's passion
for reading, but also steered her into the world of RPG's.
What began as a fun pastime, soon evolved into the creation
of fantastical worlds, but Rori never lost her love of politics
going on to specialise in Governmental History and
Historical Research.

Naturally this means her stories are steeped in historical
accuracy and real-life intrigue. While Rori's love of a happily
ever after means her preferred genre is romance, don't be
surprised if you discover an occasional detour into historical
fiction, thrillers, horror and fantasy.

ALSO BY RORI BLEU

Pineapple Meringue

Imprisoned Hearts

Port of London

Dani's Masquerade

Black Tulips

Ajei's Destiny

Porta Aeternum

The Queen's Heart

Syn *with Matthew Forester*

With Rosie Chapel

Tapestry of Shadows and Light - The Hunters Prequel

Echoes and Illusions - The Hunters: Book 1

Smoke and Mirrors - The Hunters : Book 2

Evie's War

Vindicta

Corrupt Covenant

Lesser of Two Evils

Deadly Incision

Tidbits

The Sela Helsdatter Saga

A Flip of The Coin - Book One

Conceived Chaos - Book Two

Odin's Bane - Book Three

Valhalla's Doom - Book Four

Arcane Alchemy: Freya's Fate - *A Helsdatter Saga Novella*

ALSO BY ROSIE CHAPEL

<u>Historical Fiction</u>

The Hannah's Heirloom Sequence

The Pomegranate Tree - Book One

Echoes of Stone and Fire - Book Two

Embers of Destiny - Book Three

Etched in Starlight - Prequel

Hannah's Heirloom Trilogy - Compilation — e-book only

Prelude to Fate

Legacy of Flame and Ash

The Nettleby Trilogy (WW1 Novellas)

A Guardian Unexpected - Book One

Under the Clock - Book Two

Between Heartbeats - Book Three

<u>Regency Romances</u>

The Linen and Lace Series

Once Upon An Earl - Book One

To Unlock Her Heart - Book Two

Love on a Winter's Tide - Book Three

A Love Unquenchable - Book Four

A Hidden Rose — Book Five

An Unexpected Romance

Elusive Hearts - Book One

Shrouded Hearts - Book Two

The Daffodil Garden

The Unconventional Duchess

Rescuing Her Knight - *the de Wiltons:* Book One

His Fiery Hoyden

A Regency Duet

A Regency Christmas Double

Fate is Curious

A Christmas Prayer *with Ashlee Shades*

The Lady's Wager

Winning Emma

A Love Impossible

Unravelling Roana

Love Kindled

Moonbeams and Mistletoe

The Baron's Inheritance

<u>Fairy Tale Romance</u>

Chasing Bluebells

<u>Contemporary Romances</u>

Of Ruins and Romance

All At Once It's You

Cobweb Dreams

Just One Step

His Heart's Second Sigh